AS THE NEWEST MEMBER OF AN INTERGALACTIC PEACEKEEPING
FORCE KNOWN AS THE GREEN LANTERN CORPS, HAL JORDAN
FIGHTS EVIL AND PROUDLY WEARS THE UNIFORM AND RING OF . . .

SUPER DC HEROES

GREEN LANTERN

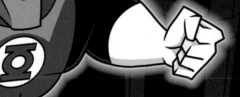

ESCAPE FROM THE ORANGE LANTERNS

WRITTEN BY
MICHAEL ACAMPORA

ILLUSTRATED BY
DAN SCHOENING

www.raintreepublishers.co.uk
Visit our website to find out
more information about
Raintree books.

To order:
☎ Phone 0845 6044371
🖶 Fax +44 (0) 1865 312263
✉ Email myorders@raintreepublishers.co.uk

Customers from outside the UK please telephone +44 1865 312262

Raintree is an imprint of Capstone Global Library Limited,
a company incorporated in England and Wales having its registered office
at 7 Pilgrim Street, London, EC4V 6LB
– Registered company number: 6695582

First published by Stone Arch Books in 2012
First published in the United Kingdom
in paperback in 2012
The moral rights of the proprietor have been asserted.

Art Directors: Bob Lentz and Brann Garvey
Designer: Hilary Wacholz
Production Specialist: Michelle Biedscheid
Editor: John-Paul Wilkins
Originated by Capstone Global Library Ltd
Printed and bound in China by Leo Paper Products Ltd

ISBN 978 1 406 23672 9 (paperback)
20 19 18 17 16 15
10 9 8 7 6 5 4 3

British Library Cataloguing in Publication Data
A full catalogue record for this book is available
from the British Library.

CONTENTS

CHAPTER 1

LOST LANTERNS

Green Lantern Hal Jordan smiled as he flew over the surface of the alien planet called Oa. The planet was at the centre of the universe and was the headquarters of the Green Lantern Corps. It was an amazing sight to behold.

Hal was on his way to meet fellow Green Lantern, Kilowog. Hal had been asked to help train some new Green Lantern recruits. Kilowog was the drill instructor on Oa, and was responsible for teaching new Lanterns how to use their power rings.

Hal had almost reached Kilowog's training grounds, when, suddenly, a green hologram popped out of his ring. It was Salaak, a fellow Green Lantern.

"Change of plans, Jordan," Salaak said. "You are to report immediately to the Guardians of the Universe at the Citadel."

The Guardians were the creators of the Green Lantern Corps. If they needed Hal's help, then something serious was about to happen.

"What's this about, Salaak?" Hal asked.

"You are going to be sent on a top secret rescue mission," explained Salaak. "The Guardians have specifically asked for your help in this matter."

Hal was honoured. "I'll be there as soon as I can!" he said.

Hal stopped in mid-air and changed direction. He blasted off towards the Guardians' headquarters.

The Guardians' Citadel sat on a large platform in the centre of Oa. The door was gigantic and made of stone. The symbol of the Green Lanterns was engraved into it.

Salaak sat at his desk outside the entrance. **CLICK! CLICK!** His many hands busily typed away at a number of computer screens. When he saw Hal arrive, he greeted him, and then opened the door to the Guardians' chamber.

As Hal walked into the chamber, he spotted another Green Lantern standing against a far wall. This Lantern looked like a wolf, but stood on two legs, and was taller than Hal.

Fendor's thick green fur stood on end. He appeared to be quite upset.

When Hal reached the centre of the room, the Guardians began to speak. "Ah, Lantern Jordan," said one of them. "Welcome."

Then another Guardian spoke. "As you may have heard from Salaak, we need your assistance on a very important mission."

"Salaak mentioned something about it being 'top secret'?" Hal said.

"Green Lanterns have been disappearing all over the universe. In the past week, the Lanterns from Space Sectors 346, 1611, 1814, and 2805 have all gone missing," a Guardian explained. "You and Lantern Fendor will investigate the disappearances and rescue the missing Lanterns."

"Fendor?" asked Hal. Before the Guardians could respond, Hal realized that Fendor must be the Green Lantern standing quietly on the other side of the chamber.

"Fendor is one of the Green Lanterns of Sector 118. His Lantern partner, Sen-Tag, has been out of contact for over ten hours. We suspect that he too has gone missing. Your search for the missing Green Lanterns will begin in Sector 118," said a Guardian. "Good luck, Lanterns. You are dismissed."

Hal and Fendor exited the Guardians' quarters. After a moment, the furry Green Lantern spoke.

"Thank you for coming with me to help find my friend, Hal Jordan," Fendor said.

"No problem," said Hal with a smile. "I'll do anything to help a fellow Lantern."

"Where exactly in Sector 118 should we begin our search?" Hal asked.

Fendor sounded upset. "I suppose we should start by investigating Sector House 118," he said. "That is where Sen-Tag's last message came from."

Fendor's suggestion made sense. In each Space Sector, there was a Sector House where Green Lanterns could rest while they were off-duty. If Sen-Tag had been there, it would be a good place to start.

"Sounds like a plan," said Hal. "Do you have any other clues?"

"After I lost contact with Sen-Tag, I flew to the Sector House," Fendor said. "As I approached it, I saw a flash of orange light through the windows. But when I reached the House, it was empty."

"A flash of orange light?" Hal said. "That's strange . . ."

"I have a feeling that the mysterious light is connected to the Lanterns' disappearances," said Fendor.

"You're probably right," Hal said. "Are you ready to head to your Sector House?"

"Yes," replied Fendor. "The sooner we can find Sen-Tag, the better."

Hal saw Fendor's tail wag nervously. "Don't worry, Fendor," Hal said. "We're going to find your friend – and the rest of the missing Lanterns."

"Thank you, Hal Jordan," Fendor answered. "I hope you are right."

With that, the Green Lanterns raised their rings into the sky. ZOOOM! Together, they blasted off into space.

CHAPTER 2

SECTOR HOUSE 118

As the Green Lanterns approached Sector House 118, Hal could see smoke billowing out of the building.

"It looks like the Sector House has been attacked," Hal said to Fendor. "Stay alert."

"Shields up," Hal told his ring. Fendor did the same.

Hal and Fendor landed inside the Sector House and began their investigation. They willed their rings to create giant green water hoses. Together, they put out the fire.

Hal looked around the house, which very much resembled a futuristic apartment. There was damage to nearly every room. Tables were broken, chairs were knocked over, and several computer screens were smashed.

In the kitchen, food had been spilled all over the floor. The fridge door had been torn off, and its shelves were empty.

In one of the bedrooms, a couple of picture frames had fallen off the walls and shattered. They showed a Green Lantern that looked like a fox, surrounded by his family. Hal realized that this must be Sen-Tag.

"It looks like a big fight took place here," Hal declared. He used his ring to put out the remaining fires.

"It does, indeed," Fendor answered. "Sen-Tag is a very powerful Lantern himself, but he and I work most effectively as a team. I was out patrolling the Sector alone when he disappeared. I should have been here to protect him."

Hal put his hand on Fendor's shoulder. "You shouldn't feel guilty," he said. "You were just doing your job. And when we rescue Sen-Tag, he'll tell you the same thing."

Fendor managed to smile at Hal's encouragement.

Hal turned to face the scene of the crime. "Now we've got to find some clue as to where your friend has gone," he said. "Do you see anything that wasn't here before? Maybe Sen-Tag's attacker left something behind . . ."

Fendor surveyed the damaged house for a moment, and then turned to Hal. "No, everything is the same – just broken and dirtier than before," Fendor said. "It looks like a dead end."

"Not quite yet, my friend," Hal said. **PHWOOT!** He used his ring to construct a big, green magnifying glass. "Ring, scan the building for anything that wouldn't normally be in a Sector House."

A minute later, Hal's ring alerted the Green Lanterns. "Scan complete," the ring chimed. "Traces of mud found. It is from a swamp on the planet Okaara in the Vega System."

Fendor's tail wagged with excitement over the discovery. "Okaara!" he exclaimed. "That must be where Sen-Tag and the missing Green Lanterns are being held!"

Hal had just opened his mouth to speak when the entire Sector House started to shake violently. **RUMMMMMMMMBLE!**

"Warning!" said the Lanterns' rings. "This structure is about to collapse!"

Pieces of the ceiling began falling down on to the Green Lanterns. Fendor created a giant umbrella with his ring to protect them from the debris.

"Let's get out of here!" Hal yelled.

The Green Lanterns made their way to the exit, but it had already crumbled into a pile of rubble. "We need to find another way out!" shouted Fendor.

"I have just the thing," yelled Hal. He held his ring out before him, creating a green bulldozer. He slammed it against the wall of the Sector House.

The bulldozer destroyed the wall, allowing the Green Lanterns to escape. They flew away from the House as quickly as they could.

Hal and Fendor watched as the Sector House exploded into millions of tiny pieces. "Sorry, Fendor," Hal said. "Looks like the Guardians will have to build you guys a new Sector House."

"That can wait," said Fendor. "First we must find Sen-Tag."

Hal nodded his head. "You're right," he said. "Next stop, Okaara!"

CHAPTER 3

PLANET OKAARA

After flying through space for several hours, Hal and Fendor finally spotted a large planet in front of them. Hal's ring alerted the Lanterns.

"Now approaching planet Okaara," said the ring.

"Finally!" said Hal with a grin. "Are you ready to find your friend?"

"I most certainly am," replied Fendor.

"Let's do this!" Hal shouted. They blasted towards the dark planet.

Within seconds, Hal and Fendor landed on the planet's surface. Okaara was a wild, overgrown jungle. There was plant life in every direction as far as the Lanterns could see. However, the sky was a smoke-coloured grey, making it look very gloomy. There were no animals on the ground, in the trees, or flying in the air.

"There doesn't seem to be any wildlife on the planet," said Hal.

"You're right," said Fendor. "My ring is showing no life signs except plants."

Hal frowned. "Something doesn't feel right about this," he said.

"According to my ring's analysis, the mud sample that led us here originated in a swamp a few miles north of our location," Fendor explained to Hal.

Fendor then pointed. "That's the way we should go –"

A green vine wrapped itself around Fendor's leg and yanked him into the air. "HELP!" he shouted.

Hal spun around. He saw a giant plant with many tentacles dangling Fendor above him. Even worse, the plant monster was holding Fendor over its mouth – a big hole filled with sharp teeth and a long, barbed tongue!

Hal had to think quickly if he was going to rescue his partner. Using his willpower, Hal imagined a machete. His power ring created a green construct that matched exactly what Hal was thinking.

Hal hacked away at the monstrous plant with the green, glowing machete. Within a matter of seconds, the tentacles had all been chopped off, and Fendor fell safely to the ground.

"That was a close one," said Fendor.

"You've got that right," said Hal. He began walking over to Fendor, but stopped when he heard a loud noise. FLAP! FLAP! Fendor was suddenly yanked into the sky again – the plant had regrown its tentacles!

Hal realized that chopping off the tentacles wasn't going to stop the vicious plant. He had to think of the best way to destroy it.

Aha! Hal thought. *There's only one way to get rid of a weed!*

Using his ring, Hal formed a construct of a giant strimmer. He held it over the plant and started its motor. *BZZT! BZZT!* The strimmer shredded the plant into thousands of pieces, freeing Fendor.

"Thank you," he said. "That was another close one."

"Hopefully the last!" Hal joked, helping Fendor to his feet. "We'll need to keep our guard up around here. This planet's plants are incredibly dangerous."

Fendor nodded. "Agreed."

The Lanterns continued following the directions of Fendor's ring. When they reached the shore of a swamp, Fendor's ring spoke. "The mud found in Sector House 118 originated here."

"What do we do now?" asked Fendor.

"Look, over there," Hal said. He pointed across the swamp. On the other bank was a large round stone with a circular symbol carved into it, which looked just like a lantern. "The Orange Lanterns are here! We must be careful."

Fendor flew to the other side of the swamp. "Hal, come here and look at this," he said.

Behind the large stone was a cave with a steep, dark staircase. They cautiously entered, using the light from the rings to guide their way.

As they travelled deeper into the cave, Fendor raised his snout and sniffed the air. "It smells terrible in here," he complained.

"Where is it coming from?" Hal asked.

"I think *that* is the cause," said Fendor.

Fendor shone his ring on a giant table in the centre of the cave. It was covered with piles of rotting meat. The smell was so disgusting that both Hal and Fendor had to pinch their noses.

"Yuck!" said Hal. "Do you think someone was planning on eating that?"

Suddenly, a voice boomed from the darkness. "Don't touch it! It's MINE!"

CHAPTER 4

THE ORANGE LANTERN

Hal and Fendor looked around for the source of the voice, but the cave was too dark to see anything. Until . . .

WHOOOOSH! WHOOOOSH! Orange pillars of light burst out of the ground. But Hal knew they weren't just beams of light. They were creatures! On the chest of each one was the same circular symbol from the cave door – the symbol of the Orange Lanterns.

Fendor turned to Hal. "What are those things?!" he asked, trembling with fear.

As the creatures emerged, Hal explained that they were orange, holographic ring constructs. The greedy minions zoomed towards the Green Lanterns, screaming the same thing in unison: "MINE!"

Hal and Fendor used their rings to create all of the weapons they could think of. The Green Lanterns swung swords, hammers, and axes, but it was no use. The orange holograms swallowed them all up! One monster with a long, spiky tail knocked Fendor on to the ground and wrapped itself around him.

"Help!" Fendor screamed.

Suddenly, a round, chubby Orange Lantern crawled up Hal's legs and grabbed him around the waist. Then, two more monstrous creatures grabbed his right and left wrists. Hal couldn't move.

The chubby creature around his waist pulled at Hal and tried to drag him away. "You belong to Glomulus now!"

"NO!" boomed the voice that had first startled the Green Lanterns. "He is MINE!" As they heard these words, the orange monsters released Hal and Fendor.

They disappeared into thin air.

A creature emerged from the darkness, emitting a sickly orange glow. He floated in front of Hal and Fendor.

He was a living, breathing monster. He had long, thin legs, and skinny arms with large, pointy claws. His face looked like a cross between a horse and a boar. His six tusks were covered in drool. He grasped an orange power battery greedily in his arms.

When Hal saw the power battery, he suddenly felt the urge to grab it away from the creature. The word "MINE!" whispered through his mind. Hal shook his head, clearing his thoughts, and was barely able to stop himself.

Then the horrible monster spoke. "Why did you interrupt MY dinner?!" it roared. "What are you doing on MY planet?!"

"You sure are greedy," Hal said. "But that's to be expected from Larfleeze, the Orange Lantern. What have you done with the missing Green Lanterns, you vile monster?"

"You're here to steal from me!" Larfleeze shouted. "You came to MY home to steal from ME!"

"Where is Sen-Tag?" cried Fendor.

Fendor tensed his muscles, preparing to attack the Orange Lantern. Hal grabbed Fendor by the shoulder. "Careful," Hal warned. "He's dangerous."

Larfleeze pointed at Fendor. "Ooh, you have a pet dog?" he asked Hal. "I WANT one!"

Fendor ignored the monster's insult. "Tell us where Sen-Tag is!" he insisted.

"Was Sen-Tag your friend, little doggy?" Larfleeze said. "Well, he's MINE now! And so are you! I'm so hungry!"

Bits of food fell from his mouth as he spoke. "My Orange Lanterns will add you to my collection!" howled the angry beast. "I'll take your shiny, green rings for myself. The more I collect, the more power I'll have!"

The wretched creature let out a disgusting belly-laugh.

"You're not taking anything from us!" shouted Hal. "You're giving us our friends back!"

"Your friends?" Larfleeze said. "Do you mean MY collection?"

Larfleeze motioned to the wall behind him, casting his orange glow upon it. There, tied up in chains, were the missing Green Lanterns. None of them wore their power rings, which were lying in a small pile on the ground. Most of the Lanterns were unconscious, but Sen-Tag managed to open one eye a little.

"Fendor," Sen-Tag said weakly. "You came to rescue me."

"Hey – I didn't say you could speak!" Larfleeze yelled as he flew over to Sen-Tag. "You're MINE now. You do what I say!"

"Leave him alone!" yelled Fendor. Hal was still holding him back, but it was getting more difficult to restrain his partner.

"Quiet!" Larfleeze roared. "I want your rings! GIMME!"

Hal stood tall in front of the Orange Lantern. "Over my dead body," he said.

Larfleeze grinned, smacking his lips. "Agreed!"

He held his battery in front of him and released dozens of orange constructs. "My Orange Lanterns will chew the rings off your fingers," he boasted. "Then they will all be MINE!"

CHAPTER 5

GREED

Orange Lanterns poured out of Larfleeze's power battery and resumed their attack on Hal and Fendor. The Green Lanterns formed a giant shield with their rings.

"He is far too powerful!" cried Fendor. "There's no way we can stop him. He will just continue to create more monsters!"

"We're not giving up," said Hal. "We have to separate him from that battery he's holding. That's how he's making all of the Orange Lanterns."

Fendor looked sceptical. "How?"

"As soon as you see a chance to rescue Sen-Tag and the others, do it," Hal said. "*I will handle Larfleeze.*"

"You are very brave," Fendor said. "Good luck, my friend."

"Same to you," Hal replied. He then ran away from the shield construct and began shouting at Larfleeze. "Hey, greedy! Do you want another ring for your collection?"

Hal raised his ring for Larfleeze to see. It caught the monster's attention, and his eyes began to glow. "Come and get it!"

"That will be MINE!" yelled Larfleeze. He was still clutching his battery in his arms, but he charged at Hal.

WHOOOOSH! Hal jumped out of the way just before the creature could grab him.

CRASH!! Larfleeze smashed through the floor of his cave instead. He tumbled down a deep hole. Hal followed.

*   *   *

When Hal reached the bottom of the hole, he thought that he was in the middle of an orange ocean. He felt around for water, but everything he touched was metal. The room that Larfleeze had landed in was filled with thousands and thousands of orange rings!

Hal spotted Larfleeze's power battery lying on the ground a few metres away from him. When he saw the battery, he again felt an intense desire to pick it up. The greedy urge was hard to resist. *Stay strong, Hal,* he told himself. *I just need to keep it away from Larfleeze long enough for the other Green Lanterns to escape.*

Larfleeze was sitting nearby on a heap of rings. He rubbed his head. "You . . . you tricked me!" he bellowed. "Just give me your ring! Why are you making this so difficult?"

"You can't have my ring, and you can't have my friends!" Hal answered.

Larfleeze stood up looking even angrier. "Don't tell me what I can't have!"

He grabbed Hal and threw him to the ground. As Hal landed, Larfleeze quickly snatched the ring off Hal's finger. Hal instantly lost all of his powers.

"Finally!" howled Larfleeze. "It's MINE!"

CLANK! A green cage formed itself around Larfleeze. Hal looked up to see Fendor, Sen-Tag, and the other rescued Green Lanterns floating above Larfleeze.

Each hero was helping to maintain the construct around the orange monster.

"Great timing!" Hal said to his friends. "I'm glad to see that you're all okay." He reached into the cage and grabbed his ring from Larfleeze. "I'll take that," he said, putting his ring back on.

Hal faced the cage. "So, how about it, Larfleeze?" he asked. "Are you willing to share your power and start helping others instead of hurting them?"

Larfleeze laughed. "Share? Help others?" the monster said. "The only person I'll ever help is myself!"

"Do you want to stay in this cave forever?" threatened Hal.

Larfleeze was grinning again. He grabbed hold of the bars of his green cage.

"I don't care!" Larfleeze said. "All of my things are here! All my rings! And my precious lantern!"

Larfleeze's words gave Hal an idea. "Have it your way," he said.

Hal created a giant green net with his ring. He snatched the Orange Lantern power battery from the ground.

"NO!" Larfleeze cried. "No – do not take my lantern! I need it! IT IS MINE!"

Hal looked Larfleeze deep in his beady, orange eyes. "You've left me with no other choice," Hal said. "I'm going to hide it on this planet. Without your powers, you'll be lucky if you ever find it."

"NOOOOOOOOO!" Larfleeze howled.

Hal flew towards the cave's exit, holding the orange battery in his hands.

Fendor and Sen-Tag followed Hal. They left Larfleeze alone and caged in his dark cave.

As Hal soared out of the mouth of the cave, he heard the battery whisper greedy things directly to his mind. *Mine,* it whispered, over and over. *MINE!*

Hal shook his head, trying to keep the voice out. *Focus, Hal,* he thought. *You only need to hold on to it for a little longer . . .*

Fendor noticed that Hal seemed pained. "Are you all right, Hal Jordan?" he asked. "You look ill."

Sen-Tag spoke up. "Yes," he agreed. "That lantern is polluting your mind with thoughts of greed, isn't it? You should get rid of it now before it consumes you."

Hal nodded at his fellow Lanterns.

"I'll hide it in the swamps," Hal said. "It will take Larfleeze ages to find it."

Fendor nodded. "An excellent plan."

Hal looked down and saw what seemed to be an endless expanse of dark, foggy swampland. The lantern was making him sick to his stomach. "This place looks as good as any," he said.

Hal and the other Lanterns hovered in place as Hal dropped the lantern. It fell like a brick, landing with a sickening **THUD!** It disappeared deep into the murky swamp.

Hal breathed a sigh of relief. He was glad to be rid of the lantern's foul influence.

Hal created a pair of green binoculars with his ring and peered through them.

Sen-Tag and Fendor did the same. "Let's release Larfleeze from his cage," Hal said.

Moments later, Larfleeze dashed out from the mouth of the cave and ran into the jungle. "Where is it?" he howled to no one at all. "WHERE IS IT?!"

"He's going the wrong way," Hal said, chuckling. "I think he'll be searching for quite some time."

"It may do him some good," Fendor added. "He will be free of the lantern's polluting influence for a while."

Hal nodded. "And who knows – perhaps Larfleeze will find *himself* in the search for his precious lantern."

"Well said, my friend," Fendor said. "Well said."

LARFLEEZE

ALIAS: Larfleeze

OCCUPATION: Orange Lantern

EYES: Orange   **HAIR:** None

POWERS/ABILITIES: Orange power ring can create constructs that can attack or defend; he can also create other Orange Lanterns to help him fight.

BIOGRAPHY

Larfleeze is the sole possessor of the Orange Lantern of avarice, or greed. A thousand years ago, Larfleeze was a member of a small group of thieves who stole valuable items from unsuspecting worlds. When they set foot on the planet Maltus, they found a priceless artefact known as the Orange Lantern power battery. Feeling its power "speak" to them, the thieves grew greedy and fought each other viciously for control of the battery. When the dust settled, only Larfleeze survived – and he has held the power battery close to his selfish heart ever since.

Larfleeze is completely consumed by greed. He trusts no one, and lives in constant fear of losing his Orange Lantern power battery – the source of his suffering as well as his powers.

As a side effect of being in constant contact with the Orange Lantern power battery, Larfleeze is overwhelmed by a hunger that makes him constantly crave more and more food.

The orange light grants its user the ability to create orange light replicas, or "constructs". Larfleeze can summon an entire army of loyal allies at will.

Hal Jordan was once able to take the Orange Lantern power ring from Larfleeze, turning him into the Orange Lantern. However, Larfleeze eventually stole it back.

BIOGRAPHIES

Michael Acampora has edited various books and magazines for DC Comics and is currently pursuing degrees in Literary Arts and Political Science at Brown University in the United States. He splits his time living with his family in New York, and friends in Rhode Island.

From an early age, **Dan Schoening** has had a passion for animation and comic books. Dan currently does freelance work in the animation and games industries and spends a lot of time with his lovely little daughter, Paige.

GLOSSARY

alerted warned someone that there might be danger

billowing smoke that is rising upwards

cautiously if you are cautious, you try hard to avoid mistakes or danger

chamber large room

collapse fall down suddenly from weakness

gloomy dull and dark

investigate search for clues to find out something

mysterious very hard to explain or understand

patrolling travelling around an area to protect it or to keep watch on people

resembled looked like something or someone

tentacle long, flexible limbs of some animals like an octopus or a squid

DISCUSSION QUESTIONS

1. This book has several characters. Which one do you like the most? Discuss your answers.

2. Hal decides to hide Larfleeze's power battery. If you were Hal, how would you have dealt with Larfleeze?

3. This book has ten illustrations. Which one is your favourite? Why?

WRITING PROMPTS

1. Larfleeze, the Orange Lantern, is greedy. Have you ever been greedy? Has anyone else ever been selfish around you? Write about your greedy experience.

2. Hal Jordan teams up with another Green Lantern to take down Larfleeze. Write about a time when you worked together with someone to get something done.

3. If you could create your own army of Orange Lanterns like Larfleeze can, what would they look like? Draw a picture of your Lantern allies, and make sure to write a brief description of each one.

MORE NEW
Green Lantern
ADVENTURES!

RED LANTERNS' REVENGE

FEAR THE SHARK

SAVAGE SANDS

PRISONER OF THE RING